how to
CODE
a sandcastle

by **Josh Funk**
illustrated by **Sara Palacios**

foreword by Reshma Saujani, founder of Girls Who Code

VIKING

FOREWORD

Hi, I'm Reshma, and I'm the founder of Girls Who Code.

Do you know what coding is? As you'll discover in this book, it's basically how humans tell a computer—or a robot—what to do. But it's also about using creativity and imagination to define, explore, and solve problems of all kinds.

Girls Who Code is an organization that wants to teach every girl to learn to code! And you don't have to wait until middle school or later to introduce girls to coding. Just like kids begin to learn about subjects like animals, history, and space before they get to kindergarten, we want to make coding a familiar part of every child's world. By introducing the core concepts of coding to children now, we're helping prepare them for a future of changing the world through code.

Happy reading—and coding!

Reshma Saujani

Hello, World, I'm Pearl.

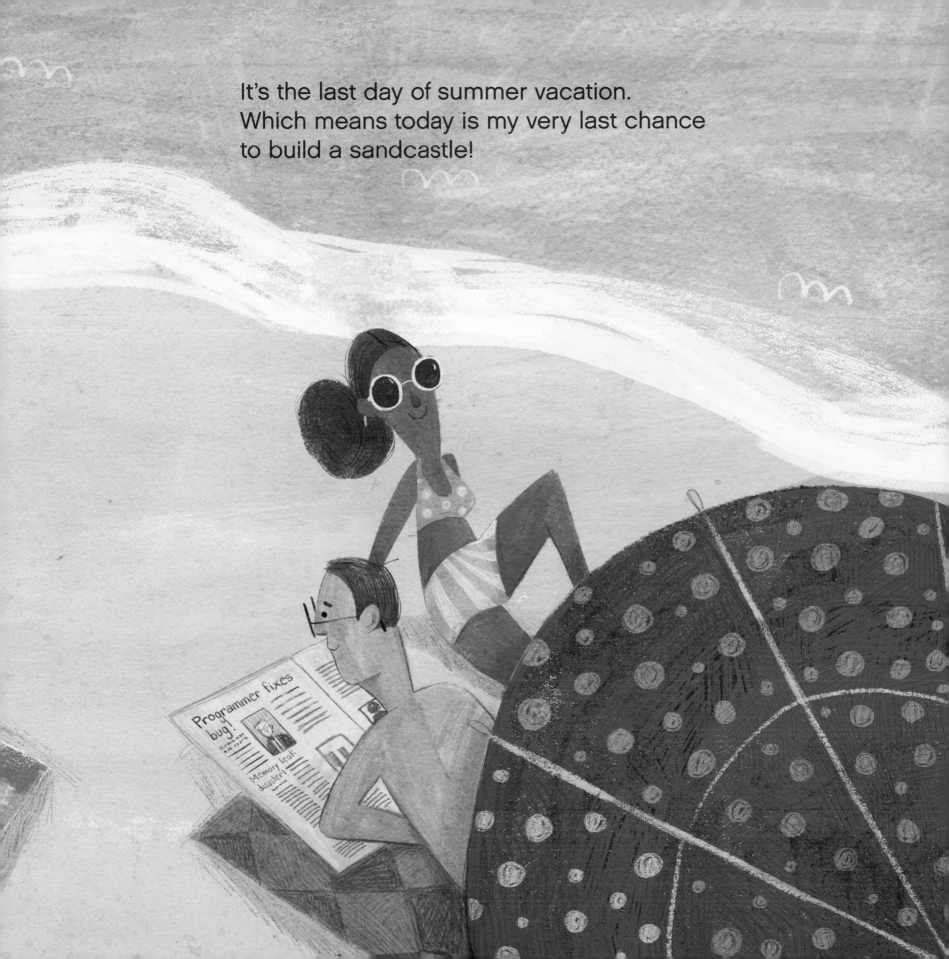

It's the last day of summer vacation.
Which means today is my very last chance
to build a sandcastle!

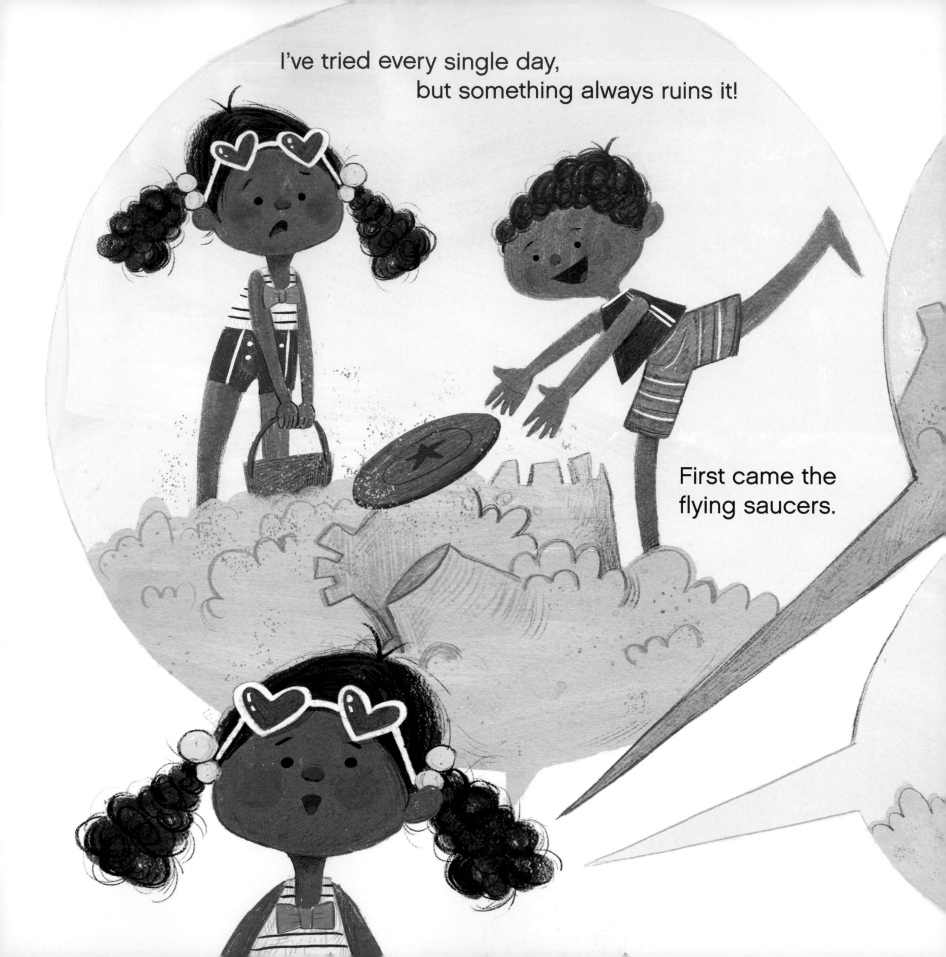

I've tried every single day,
but something always ruins it!

First came the
flying saucers.

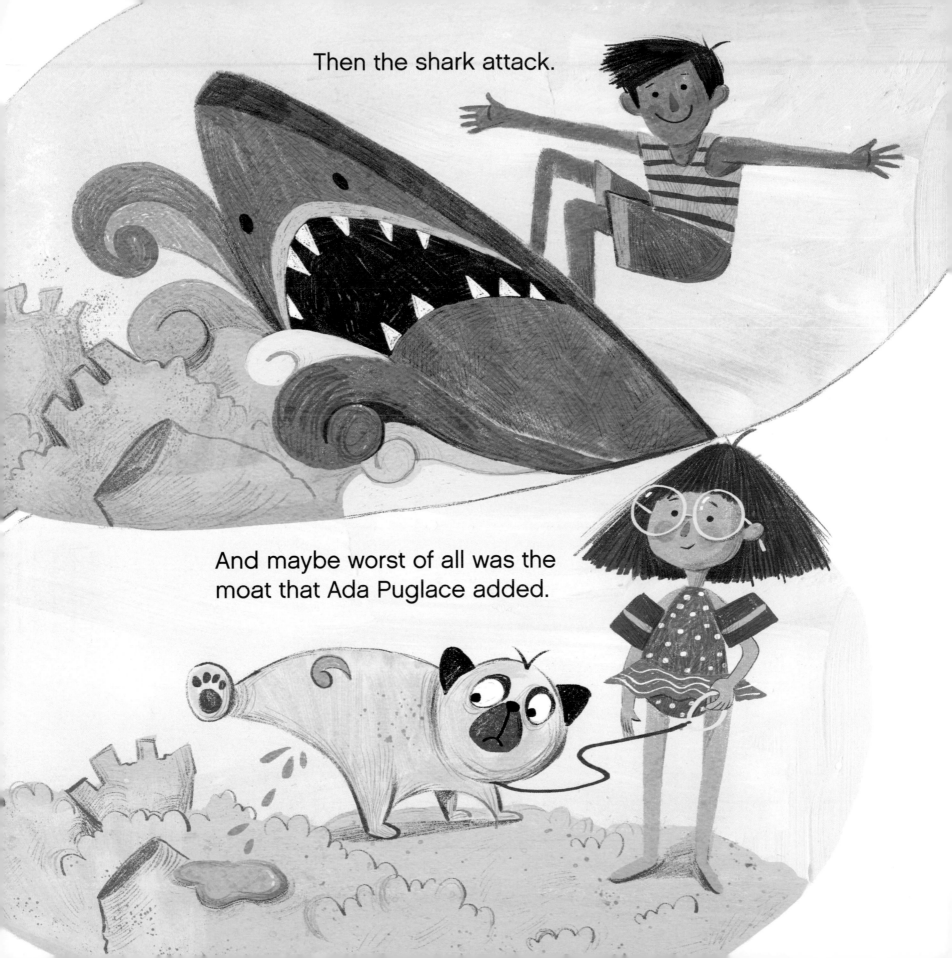

Then the shark attack.

And maybe worst of all was the
moat that Ada Puglace added.

But today, I've got the perfect plan. I've brought my trusty rust-proof robot, Pascal.

He'll do whatever I tell him—as long as I tell him in CODE. It's not a *secret code*—it's special instructions that computers understand.

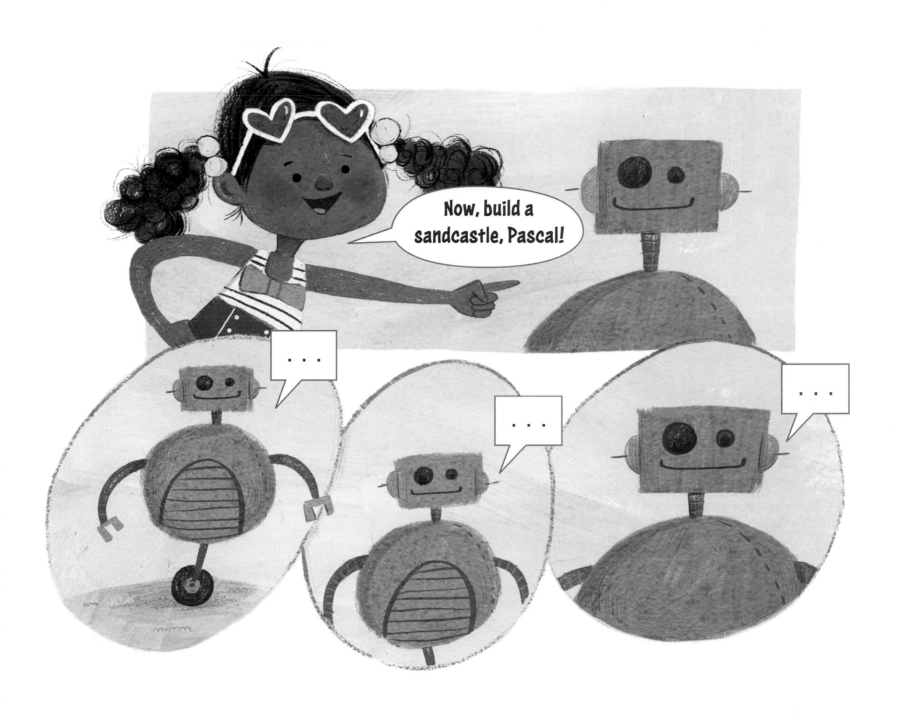

Hmm. I guess he doesn't know how to do that. But a coder takes one *big* problem and breaks it into several *smaller* ones. If I give Pascal enough instructions that he *does* know, we'll build this castle in no time! It'll be easy!

I guess I need to be very specific with my instructions.

Pascal, find a flat spot on sand that isn't too close to the water.

This isn't as easy as I thought.
But at least we have a place to build.

SMALL PROBLEM #2: GATHER UP SAND

Now we'll need a *huge* pile of sand.
It's *very* important to tell Pascal everything in the correct **SEQUENCE**—
that means in the right order.

1. Fill the pail
   with sand.

2. Dump the sand
   on our spot.

3. Pat the
   sand down.

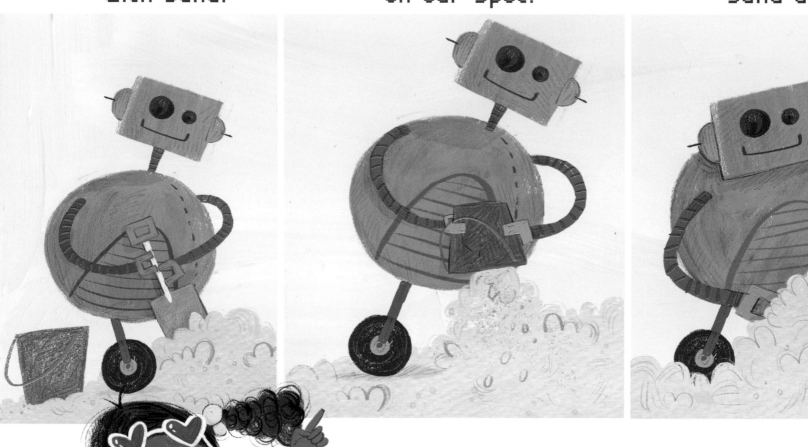

Great job, Pascal! Now let's do it again.

There must be a coding trick I can use.
Aha! A **LOOP**!
When you need to repeat something in code,
you can use a **LOOP**!

Let's each find some fancy decorations and bring them back here.

Maybe I need to give him better instructions. An **IF-THEN-ELSE** should do the trick.

IF the item you see is small and doesn't move and doesn't belong to anyone

THEN bring the item back to the castle

ELSE find something different

Perfect!
Let's shape the castle and decorate.

A moat would have protected the castle from the tide! If only I had thought of a moat earlier. It took half the day to figure out how to **CODE** a sandcastle . . .

But hold on. I already wrote the **CODE** to build a sandcastle. I can easily use all that **CODE** again!

1. Find a place to build.

I think a new **SEQUENCE** should solve this small problem. And I know how to write one of those. Let's try:

1. Dig around the outside of the castle.

2. Fill the pail with sand.

3. Empty the pail away from the castle.

And we need to repeat that until we've gone all around the castle. I know—another **LOOP**!

Hurray! Our sandcastle is finished and safe from the ocean! Let's play!

Hey, Pascal, now that we know how
to CODE one sandcastle . . .

We can
code an
entire KINGDOM!

return(); // THE END

for each (girl$_n$ in AllGirls), StartLoop:
   print ("This book is for ", girl$_n$, NewLine);
:EndLoop

—J.F.

To the girls who code and the girls who draw.
—S.P.

VIKING
Penguin Young Readers
An imprint of Penguin Random House LLC
375 Hudson Street
New York, New York 10014

First published in the United States of America by Viking,
an imprint of Penguin Random House LLC, 2018

LIBRARY OF CONGRESS CATALOGING-IN-PUBLICATION DATA IS AVAILABLE
ISBN: 9780425291986

Printed in China   Designed by Kate Renner

4   5   6   7   8   9   10

The illustrations for this book were rendered digitally
in combination with gouache and acrylic paintings.

Pearl and Pascal's Guide to Coding

WHAT IS CODE?

Code is the set of instructions a computer uses to do any type of task, such as solving a problem.

Sometimes these tasks and problems can seem really big, so one thing coders do is break difficult big problems into smaller, easier ones. Rather than build an entire sandcastle, which is a difficult big task, Pearl decided to think of it as several smaller, easier tasks.

WHAT IS A SEQUENCE?

Code must be written in a specific order called a sequence. Just like a story wouldn't make sense if the sentences were rearranged in the wrong order, code won't work if it's written in the wrong sequence.

For example, if a story is told as follows:
    Pearl wakes up.
    Pearl eats breakfast.
    Pearl gets dressed.
    Pearl goes to school.
That makes perfect sense.

However, if the order of the sentences is changed:
    Pearl eats breakfast.
    Pearl wakes up.
    Pearl goes to school.
    Pearl gets dressed.
The story no longer makes sense (and introduces many questions: Does Pearl eat breakfast in her sleep? Does she go to school in her pajamas?).

Pearl and Pascal's Guide to Coding

WHAT IS A LOOP?

One common coding technique is a loop. A loop helps when you want to repeat a sequence. Instead of writing the sequence over and over again, you write it only once— inside of a loop.

WHAT IS AN IF-THEN-ELSE?

An if-then-else is sort of like answering a *true or false* question. If the answer is true, then you do one thing. If it's false, you do something else. Sometimes this is called a *conditional*.

In the story, Pascal keeps finding inappropriate decorations. Pearl uses an if-then-else to get Pascal to check whether the item is okay before bringing it back. If the item fits Pearl's rules, then Pascal can bring it back. Otherwise, Pascal will keep looking for something else.